STRANGER THINGS

THE OTHER SIDE #4

NETFLIX
STRANGER THINGS
THE OTHER SIDE #4

script
JODY HOUSER

pencils
STEFANO MARTINO

inks
KEITH CHAMPAGNE

colors
LAUREN AFFE

lettering
NATE PIEKOS OF BLAMBOT®

front cover art by
ALEKSI BRICLOT

ABDO Spotlight

DARK HORSE BOOKS

ABDOBOOKS.COM

Reinforced library bound edition published in 2020 by Spotlight, a division of ABDO, PO Box 398166, Minneapolis, Minnesota 55439. Spotlight produces high-quality reinforced library bound editions for schools and libraries.
Published by agreement with Dark Horse Comics.

Printed in the United States of America, North Mankato, Minnesota.
042019
092019

Library of Congress Control Number: 2019939089

Publisher's Cataloging-in-Publication Data

Names: Houser, Jody, author. | Martino, Stefano; Champagne, Keith; Affe, Lauren, illustrators.
Title: The other side / writer: Jody Houser; art: Stefano Martino; Keith Champagne; Lauren Affe.
Description: Minneapolis, Minnesota: Spotlight, 2020 | Series: Stranger things
Summary: This spine-tingling comic based on the hit Netflix series follows Will Byers' struggle to survive in the treacherous Upside Down.
Identifiers: ISBN 9781532143878 (#1; lib. bdg.) | ISBN 9781532143885 (#2; lib. bdg.) | ISBN 9781532143892 (#3; lib. bdg.) | ISBN 9781532143908 (#4; lib. bdg.)
Subjects: LCSH: Stranger things (Television program)--Juvenile fiction. | Science fiction television programs--Juvenile fiction. | Supernatural disappearances--Juvenile fiction. | Monsters--Juvenile fiction. | Graphic novels--Juvenile fiction. | Comic books, strips, etc.--Juvenile fiction
Classification: DDC 741.5--dc2

Spotlight

A Division of ABDO
abdobooks.com

MINUTES AGO, WILL BYERS HAD HOPE.
IT WASN'T THE FIRST TIME HE'D FOUND IT IN THIS STRANGE WORLD. IT WASN'T THE FIRST TIME HE'D LOST IT.
A FAMILIAR FACE, A SOOTHING VOICE IN THE WALL.
LIGHT AND SAFETY SHINING OUT OF A TREE.
NOW THERE IS ONLY DARKNESS AND THE MONSTERS THAT IT HOLDS.
AND HOW LONG HE CAN KEEP ONE STEP AHEAD, HE DOESN'T KNOW.

HE SUSPECTS THAT IT MAY NOT BE FOR MUCH LONGER.
THE AIR... GETTING HARDER TO BREATHE.
THOUGHT I WAS GETTING USED TO IT.
MAYBE I JUST NEED TO REST...

WILL IS AWARE OF TIME PASSING AS HE MOVES THROUGH THE WOODS. OF THINGS CHANGING.
HOW MUCH OF EITHER, THOUGH, HE CAN'T SAY.
THERE IS LESS AND LESS HE'S SURE OF HERE IN THE DARK.

ALL HE KNOWS IS THAT THIS STRANGE WORLD IS GROWING EVEN STRANGER.
AND HIS STRENGTH IS FLAGGING.

WHAT HE SEES BEFORE HIM IS LIKELY A TRICK. EITHER OF THIS PLACE, OR HIS OWN MIND.
CASTLE BYERS

FALLING FOR IT WOULDN'T BE VERY WISE AT ALL.

BUT HE HAS FEW OPTIONS NOW. THERE WILL BE NO MORE RUNNING.

THE ONLY WAY HE WILL SURVIVE IS TO FIND SHELTER. A SAFE PLACE.

A HOME AWAY FROM HOME.

FOR THE MOMENT, HE IS SAFE.
AND CLOSER TO BEING FOUND THAN HE EVER REALIZED.
WILL.
WHO...

WILL?

YOUR MOM...
...SHE'S COMING FOR YOU.
HURRY.

CASTLE BYERS
HURRY.

JUST... JUST HOLD ON A LITTLE LONGER.

WILL.
WILL.
AND ONCE MORE, WILL THE WISE IS LEFT ALONE.
HE KNOWS HE SHOULD BE CURIOUS WHO THIS OTHER-WORDLY FIGURE WAS.
HOPEFUL THAT HIS MOTHER IS COMING.
SCARED THAT SHE WON'T ARRIVE IN TIME.
ALL FRIENDS ARE
HOME OF WILL THE
CASTLE BYERS
BUT HE DOESN'T HAVE IT IN HIM TO FEEL MUCH OF ANYTHING AT ALL IN THE MOMENT.

THIS PLACE HAS TAKEN EVERYTHING FROM HIM.
ALMOST.
...IF I STAY...
...TROUBLE...

THE SONG MAY GIVE HIM STRENGTH, AS IT HAS IN THE PAST.

BUT IT ALSO SERVES AS A BEACON.

AND BY THE TIME HE REALIZES THAT...
...I GO NOW

...IT'S ALREADY TOO LATE.
SKRRRR

SKRRR

SKREEE
SKREEE
"ARE YOU SCARED?"

NO. IT'S JUST A STUPID BOOK.
I HEARD HIS BOOKS WERE REALLY SCARY.

YEAH, BUT THOSE ARE ABOUT MONSTERS AND HORROR STUFF.
THIS ONE'S SUPPOSED TO BE A FANTASY, RIGHT?
I THOUGHT MAYBE I COULD GET SOME COOL IDEAS FOR THE NEXT CAMPAIGN.

MAYBE YOU COULD ASK MISS MARISSA?
YEAH, RIGHT.

SHE'D PROBABLY CALL MY MOM AND TELL HER I WAS READING INAPPROPRIATE STUFF.

WOULD YOU REALLY GET IN TROUBLE FOR JUST ASKING ABOUT A BOOK?
WORSE.
MY MOM'S ALL INTO SITTING DOWN AS A FAMILY AND TALKING ABOUT OUR FEELINGS AND CRAP NOW.

I COULD SNEAK IT INTO MY HOUSE. MY MOM WOULDN'T CARE.

...I DON'T MEAN IT LIKE THAT. OF COURSE SHE *CARES.*
SHE'S JUST REALLY BUSY WORKING EXTRA SHIFTS. I DON'T THINK SHE'D NOTICE.

HEY, YOUR MOM IS PRETTY COOL.
I MEAN, SHE'S STILL A MOM. BUT SHE KIND OF *GETS* IT, YOU KNOW?
YEAH. OR AT LEAST SHE TRIES.

I BET I COULD READ A FEW CHAPTERS BEFORE BABY HOLLY IS DONE WITH STORYTIME.

BESIDES, IF *YOU* READ IT, IT COULD SPOIL THE CAMPAIGN.
YOU GOT ME. I'M JUST LOOKING OUT FOR WILL THE WISE.

PUBLIC LIBRARY
"I WANT HIM TO LIVE FOREVER."
IT IS DEEP IN THE NEST OF THE MONSTER THAT WILL FINALLY REGAINS HIS SENSES.
WIIIILL...
CAN'T... CAN'T MOVE...

VERY QUICKLY, HE WISHES HE HADN'T.
DARLING.

YOU STAYED.

SUCH COLD EYES.

WE HEARD YOUR SONG.

AND NOW YOU'RE RIGHT WHERE YOU BELONG.

THE CLOTHES FIT NOW.
WE KNOW WHO YOU ARE.
WHO YOU'RE SUPPOSED TO BE.
HERE WITH US.
IN THE BLACK.
'TIL THE END OF TIME.
WE'RE HERE.
WE'RE ALWAYS HERE.
YOU **WILL** STAY.

WIIIIIILL...
WIIIIIIIIIIILL...
WILL! WILL!
WILL! OH MY GOD!
YOU NEED TO HELP ME GET HIM OUT!
...MOM...
GET HIM OUT!

THERE IS NO SENSE OF ANYTHING FOR A WHILE. OF TIME OR PLACE OR PEOPLE.

YOU'RE HOME.
YOU'RE HOME NOW.
YOU'RE SAFE.

JUST... JUST SEEING THINGS.
JONATHAN.
YEAH. IT'S ME, BUDDY.

WE MISSED YOU.

WE REALLY MISSED YOU.
"IT GOT ME."

THE DEMOGORGON.
WE KNOW. IT'S OKAY.
IT'S DEAD.

"WE MADE A NEW FRIEND.
"SHE STOPPED IT.

"SHE SAVED US."

BUT SHE'S GONE NOW.

AND WILL BYERS IS LEFT TO WONDER.
IS IT REALLY OVER?
CAN ANYONE TRULY FACE A DEMOGORGON AND EMERGE UNSCATHED?
THE END